To the Forsg

Dorothy Nelson

STENCH

Written by
DOROTHY HAYES NELSON

Illustrated by
SURIAH SCHOTT

Dorothy's Ditties
Publishing

Mesa, Arizona

STENCH
By Dorothy Hayes Nelson

Published by:
Dorothy's Ditties Publishing
Mesa, Arizona

First edition Hardcover Printing copyright © 2016, Dorothy Nelson

ISBN 13: 978-1-944826-29-1

1- Fiction   2- Children's Story   3- Picture Books

Illustrator Credit: Suriah Schott

Photography Credits:
Allison Tyler Jones Photography, Inc.
166 W Main Street Suite #103, Mesa, AZ 85201
Studio: 480.584.5267
Cell: 480.593.3079
Website http://www.atjphoto.com/
Blog http://www.atjphoto.com/blog
Instagram: @ATJPHOTO
Twitter: @ATJPHOTO
Facebook: Allison Tyler Jones Photography, Inc.

Interior Page Design and Cover finished by Patti Hultstrand

Printed in the United States of America

DEDICATION

To all my grand-darlings, who make life worthwhile.

ACKNOWLEDGEMENTS

To my grade one through twelve teachers who inspired me to be a teacher.

INTRODUCTION

I was inspired to write this book while sitting on the front porch of our cabin and seeing twelve tiny skunks playing in the front yard of our neighbor across the street, who did not even know they had been born under her storage shed. They were so darling and thought they were as big as anybody.

Stench was the eldest of twelve skunks

born under the storage shed belonging to Mrs. Hayes.

It was a wonderful home.

His mother had carefully dug out a large hollow on the north side,

and she had lined her den with her own soft fur from her tummy.

His mother worked very hard to feed her little ones.

Not only did they get warm milk from her own body,

but she walked long distances to find them other food—

especially as they grew older and needed more and more food.

Stench was growing up.

He could feel it in a certain restlessness

when he awakened in the morning,

stretched, and sniffed the warm breeze outside.

Then he would find his mother

and ask her if he could please go outside.

"Not yet, Stench," she would patiently answer.

"Don't be too anxious to grow up.

It can be dangerous outside.

There are hawks and owls that eat little skunks.

Cars go by on the road very swiftly—

that's how you lost your cousin, Willie,

because he went outside while his mother

was hunting for food and a car hit him.

You must learn about danger before you can go outside."

"Look, Mother," Stench would answer,

"see how strong my legs are and how well I can lift my tail?"

"Just having strong legs and being able to lift your tail

are not enough for a young skunk."

His mother would say quietly, "Be patient, Stench."

Stench thought of some of the delicious meals they had shared in their snug little home.

He remembered scrambled eggs with bacon grease and biscuits that Mrs. Walsh had put out after breakfast.

When he mentioned it to Smelly,

he recalled fresh cantaloupe.

Aroma heard them talking and said her favorite

was strawberry jam on whole wheat toast with butter.

Odor piped up that steak and mashed potatoes

with salad got her vote.

Scent then reminded them of the time the Nobles

had to leave right after a birthday party

and they got cake with whipped cream frosting and ice cream.

He had a sweet tooth and loved desserts.

Stinker closed her eyes and sighed as she remembered

the family reunion across the street.

It had been Fourth of July

and they'd had corn-on-the-cob with hot dogs.

Cologne loved fancy dishes

and her favorite was the time their mother

had brought leftover filet mignon with mushrooms.

Pauly's eyes danced as he reminded them of the day

Charlie burned the bottom on a pan of enchiladas

and just set the entire pan out to cool.

They had a feast!

Perfume's fondest memory was for the

chocolate-dipped strawberries with real whipped cream.

Chantel was the family health nut and fondly thought

of the time the Vegan campers left veggie burgers

with sprouts and avocado.

Sulfur had to mention the time the broccoli truck turned over—

he even loved the smell of broccoli.

STENCH

Garlic set them all to dreaming when she recalled

the leftovers from an Italian Restaurant—

specifically that Alfredo sauce.

It suddenly got quiet in their den as each little skunk enjoyed

remembering delicious feasts from the past.

Then Stench spoke up.

"That's why we've got to get out of here. We'll have our choices

of all the great food when we can leave this den

and go out into the world. We can just step outside

and follow our noses to whatever kind of food we want!"

"Mother," tattled Cologne.

"Stench wants to go outside,

and he knows we're

not allowed."

"Stench," warned Mrs. Skunk, "you know that I must decide if you're ready to go out into the world."

"Yes, Mother," Stench answered meekly, but he glared at Cologne. Then he made up his mind that he would show them all that he was ready.

Stench awoke early the next morning. He carefully left the warm

nest they all made by snuggling together.

He knew he mustn't disturb the others.

He looked at each face to make sure they were all still asleep—

particularly his mother.

Gentle snores came from several, and all eyes were closed.

Smelly stirred a bit and sighed as he dreamed.

"Now is my chance," thought Stench.

He ran his sharp claws through his

black and white fur as he had been

taught to do to groom himself for the day.

He rubbed his beady black eyes

to make sure no sleep was left.

He ran his pink tongue over his fine,

white teeth to clean them.

Then he stuck his nose up

into the opening of their den and sniffed.

Oh, it smelled wonderful outside.

As soon as he got out he would be free!

Stench thought about the food he would find.

He knew it would be so much fun to be his own boss—

no one telling him what to do.

There would be no one crowded against him,

he would not have to share what he found—

he could eat it all himself.

He could sit in the sunshine and warm his shiny fur.

Maybe he would even find other animals to talk with.

He hurried quietly up into the summer morning.

The air was warm,

but there was a nice breeze.

It brought the smell

of bacon and eggs.

Stench stepped onto the cool, green grass,

and dug his claws into it—it felt so good.

He stretched his body and then each leg,

as he admired his shiny coat.

Maybe he would just follow his nose

and have bacon and eggs for breakfast.

He made his way around the corner of Mrs. Hayes's house

and was completely unprepared for her dog, Brute.

Brute jumped up and began barking ferociously.

Stench was so frightened that he forgot the way back home

and ran quickly across the street.

He even forgot to lift his tail.

Thank goodness Brute had been chained up.

Halfway across the street, Stench was very surprised

when a delivery truck swerved to avoid hitting him.

But he could feel the very air

strike his body from the movement of the truck.

Then Stench remembered his mother's warning about cars.

He knew he wouldn't get bacon and eggs with Brute

guarding the house so closely,

so he began wandering around the house across the street.

His nose told him that there were biscuits and gravy nearby,

but when he found them, there were ants all over

and the food smelled rather spoiled.

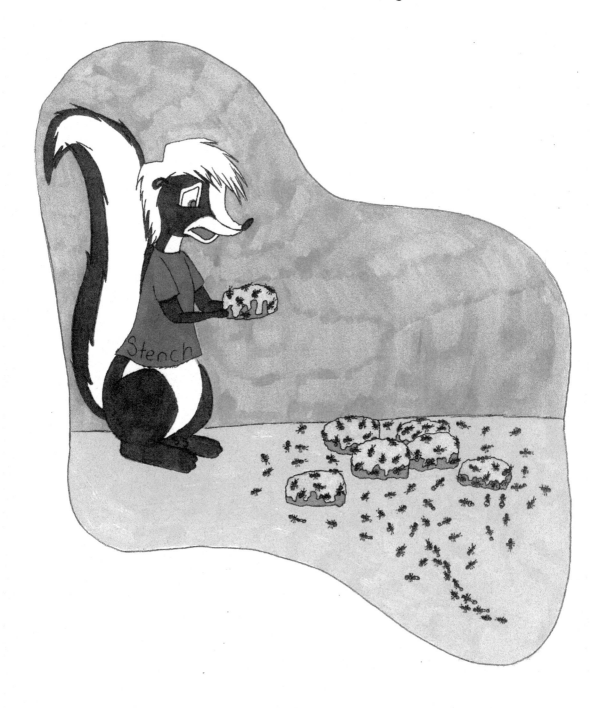

Stench ate the food, but he remembered

how fresh and clean the food was

that his mother brought for them,

and he felt ashamed to be eating all of this without sharing.

He began to realize how far his mother must sometimes

travel to find such fresh, delicious food for them all.

Twelve skunks eat a lot!

Stench saw a bird feeder hanging in a tree, and knew that seeds

often fell out when the birds ate and he could enjoy a few.

He walked to the tree and right under the feeder

he saw seeds of several kinds that he could eat,

but before he could choose even one seed,

a big bluejay screamed in his ear

and swooped down to dive bomb him.

The jay didn't actually touch him,

but he was so frightened he covered his eyes

and waited for the pain.

Then the cheeky bluejay landed in the tree

and made fun of scared little Stench.

Stench had had enough!

He cautiously walked back to the street.

He looked both ways to be sure no vehicles were coming.

He looked around and made sure he knew

on which side of the house Brute was tied,

and he walked clear around on the other side of the shed.

How happy Stench was when he saw the opening

that led down to their snug home!

The warm sun and soft grass didn't seem so important now.

What seemed important was getting home

and seeing his family again.

He wouldn't even mind when his sisters wanted

to play house and he had to be the baby.

Stench hurried down into the den.

He checked carefully to make sure everyone was still asleep.

It seemed like such a long time since he left.

No one else was awake, so Stench checked himself

to make sure he was still in one piece,

then snuggled up next to Chantel

and quietly dropped off to sleep.

He was awakened later

when his mother brought fresh bacon and eggs,

but no one understood why Stench wasn't hungry.

All day long he played happily with his brothers and sisters.

After a supper of hamburgers and fries,

his mother gave them sweet red grapes,

then she said she needed to talk with them.

"I've been watching you for weeks now," she said,

"and I believe you're ready to go outside

and play for the first time."

"You must be careful to stay on this side of the house,

because Brute is tied on the other.

Please do not try to cross the road until later.

You must learn to watch for cars or you could be killed.

You all know that when we find food, we share with everyone.

Now, be careful and have fun together.

I will call you when it's time to come in."

Everyone grinned because they knew they were big now,

and would soon be finding their own dens.

But, before he left, Stench said,

"Mother, are you sure we're ready?"

ABOUT THE AUTHOR:

I was raised on a dairy farm with three sisters and one brother. I attended the excellent Peoria Public Schools, where I made up my mind in seventh grade that I wanted to be a teacher. I have loved writing, and won some prizes for it during those years, and I was salutatorian when I graduated from eighth grade. I began college at the U of A, in Tucson, where I met my husband. I graduated with a B.A. in elementary education from ASU and began teaching in the Mesa Public Schools. I later earned an M.A. in secondary education with an emphasis in history from NAU.

We have three wonderful children, Jenni, married to Rob Ferrin is the mother of seven and graduated from NAU. Paul graduated from ASU and is married to Ashley, and they have two children. Alicia graduated from BYU, is married to David King, and they have four children. All of the grandchildren are extraordinary—a totally unbiased opinion!

I live in Mesa with my attorney husband, and still enjoy being in the classroom as a substitute. I love doing counted cross stitch, regular embroidery, reading, baking, doing puzzles, and being a grandma.

Contact info: e-mail me at gabbyd327@gmail.com

CPSIA information can be obtained
at www.ICGtesting.com
Printed in the USA
LVOW06*0719260217

525443LV00004B/4/P

9 781944 826262